My Garden of
FLOWER FAiRiES

My Garden of
FLOWER FAIRIES

CICELY MARY BARKER

FREDERICK WARNE

FREDERICK WARNE

Published by the Penguin Group
Penguin Books Ltd, 80 Strand, London WC2R 0RL, England
Penguin Putnam Inc., 375 Hudson Street, New York, New York 10014, USA
Penguin Books Australia Ltd, 250 Camberwell Road, Camberwell, Victoria 3124, Australia
Penguin Books Canada Ltd, 10 Alcorn Avenue, Toronto, Ontario, Canada M4V 3B2
Penguin Books India (P) Ltd, 11 Community Centre,
Panchsheel Park, New Delhi 110 017, India
Penguin Books (NZ) Ltd, Cnr Rosedale and Airborne Roads, Albany, Auckland, New Zealand
Penguin Books (South Africa) (Pty) Ltd, P O Box 9, Parklands 2121, South Africa

Penguin Books Ltd, Registered Offices: 80 Strand, London WC2R 0RL, England

Web site at: www.flowerfairies.com

First published by Frederick Warne 2003
This edition first published 2003
10 8 6 4 2 1 3 4 5 7 9

This edition copyright © Frederick Warne & Co., 2003
New reproductions of Cicely Mary Barker's illustrations copyright
© The Estate of Cicely Mary Barker, 1990
Copyright in original text and illustrations © The Estate of Cicely Mary Barker, 1923, 1925,
1926, 1934, 1940, 1944, 1948, 1985

ISBN 0 7232 4926 1

Printed in Hong Kong

Contents

Welcome 10

Daisy 12

Marigold 14

Periwinkle 16

Candytuft 18

Daffodil 20

Tulip 22

Rose 24

Lavender 26

Poppy 28

Snapdragon 30

Sweet Pea 32

Nasturtium 34

Heather 36

Iris 38

Honeysuckle 40

Nightshade 42

Michaelmas Daisy 44

Welcome...

...to the garden where the Flower Fairies live! A Flower Fairy's job is to look after her plant, polishing leaves and trimming flowers. A Flower Fairy is 5 – 10 centimetres (2 – 4 inches) tall, and has a pair of delicate wings. She, although a Flower Fairy can be a boy too, dresses in the leaves and flowers from her plant to help her stay hidden. A Flower Fairy is not at all fussy about where she lives. Hanging baskets, window-boxes, a tiny crack in a crumbling wall or between the pavement stones where weeds and mosses grow – any of these places might be home to a Flower Fairy. Since almost everyone has a potted plant, or can see a patch of grass, or treetops from their window, this means that almost everyone is close to a Flower Fairy even if they don't realise it at the time!

The Pink Fairies are trimming the petals of their flowers

This book is about a group of Flower Fairies who live in a very big garden. The flower beds are dense with pretty plants that flower at different times of the year. Here the Flower Fairies live crowded together in sociable groups, cheerfully chattering and playing. There is a rose garden, where lavender is planted to attract the butterflies. Other parts of this garden are so overgrown that nobody has walked there for years – down by the stream there are reeds and rushes choking the water, the trees hang over, and the hedges are woody through lack of pruning. Here the Flower Fairies are wilder, and less friendly…

Lavender clutches a stem and sways in the breeze

Iris wears a dress made from the petals of her plant

Daisy

At the edge of the lawn, the sun rises.
Daisy Fairy's petals open wide to
greet the day. She is the 'day's eye'
watching the little fairies through
the daylight hours. She picks
some of her blossoms to make
a daisy chain and calls to all
the youngest fairies to
gather inside the circle,
they will stay there while
the older fairies go about their
daily chores. In the evening,
her petals close, signalling
that it is bedtime for the
baby fairies.

The youngest fairies are here to play

Black Medic talks to her little brother

Little Herb Robert

Young Dandelion

Baby Forget-me-not

Daisy has made her circle of flowers

Baby Wood Sorrel

13

Marigold

In the flower bed, Marigold takes up the sunniest spot.
Her petals open up to greet the sun in the morning and
close again when the sun goes down. During the day,
Marigold takes no notice of her fairy friends,
even though they try to persuade her to play
with them. Instead, Marigold perches happily
on a flower and soaks up the sunshine.

The Crocus Fairies laugh and shout, but Marigold pays no attention

Laburnum sunbathes too

Great Sun above me in the sky, so golden glorious, and high,

My petals, see, are golden too, they shine, but cannot shine like you.

It is because I love you so, I turn to watch you as you go

Without your light, no joy could be. Look down, great Sun, and shine on me!

Chilly Winter Aconite
basks in the sun

Periwinkle

Under trees and in the shady places in the garden, Periwinkle spreads his little blue flowers and dark green leaves. When Periwinkle is feeling mischievous, he uses the prickly edges around his leaves to tickle the other fairies' feet.

Periwinkle tickles Pansy's toes

Pansy almost loses her grip

16

Weee! Spindle Berry holds on tight

But Periwinkle has a more serious job in the garden – he makes tough string from the stalks of his plant. The fairies use the string for many things, but what they like to use the string for most, is swinging from plant to plant!

Robin Pincushion is having fun!

Silver Birch is a dazzling acrobat

Candytuft

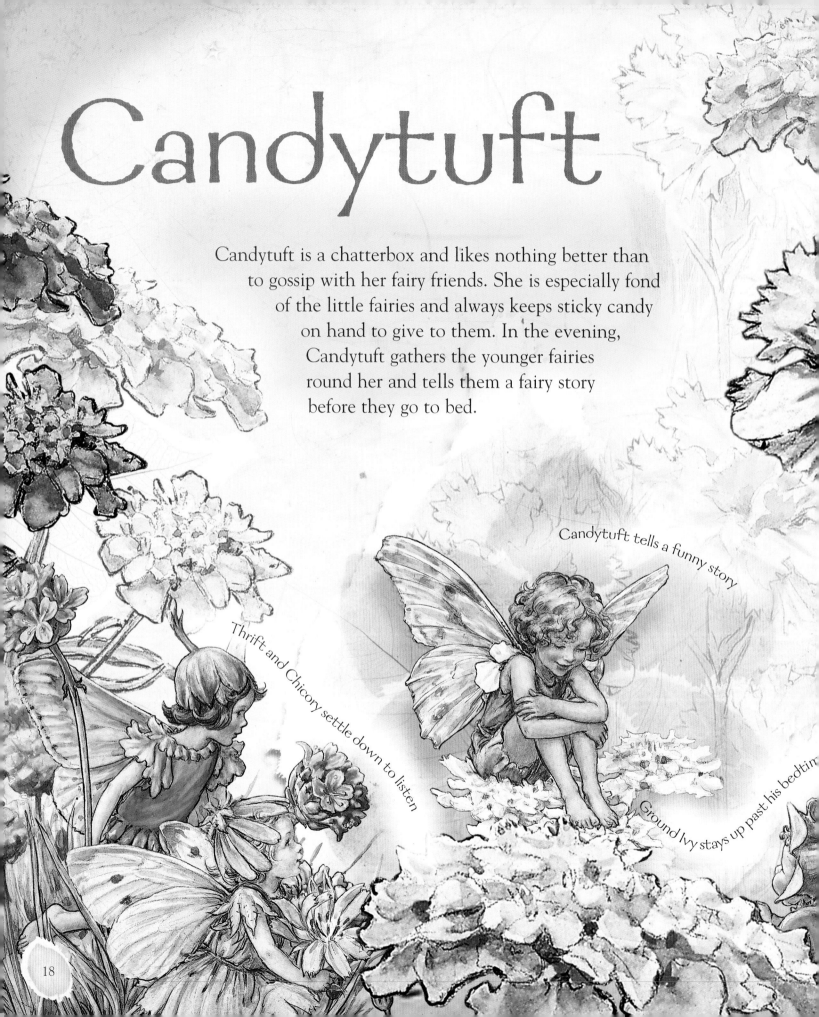

Candytuft is a chatterbox and likes nothing better than to gossip with her fairy friends. She is especially fond of the little fairies and always keeps sticky candy on hand to give to them. In the evening, Candytuft gathers the younger fairies round her and tells them a fairy story before they go to bed.

Candytuft tells a funny story

Thrift and Chicory settle down to listen

Ground Ivy stays up past his bedtim

18

Shy Bindweed listens quietly

19

Daffodil

When the garden fairies have time to spare, they play games. Daffodil is especially good at hide-and-seek because none of the other fairies can ever find her. This is because Daffodil becomes invisible. She stands quietly by her flower as the other fairies search high and low for her.

"Where are you Daffodil?" shouts Narcissus

The Crocus Fairies can't find Daffodil anywhere!

Just as her fairy friends are about to give up, Daffodil re-appears!

Tulip

The busy flower beds are home to some exotic Flower Fairies.
Tulip is a visitor from the land of Persia. It didn't take Tulip long
to make friends with the other fairies in the garden as she is always
polite. Tulip also tells great stories about faraway lands.
Whenever fairies are feeling sad, they come to Tulip for advice.
And because Tulip is wise and has seen a great many
things, she always has good advice to give.

Buttercup wishes that she could go to faraway places

Michaelmas listens intently to Tulip's wise words

My stalks are very straight and tall,
My colours clear and bright
Too many-hued to name them all—
Red, yellow, pink, or white.

Little
Scilla
listens, too

23

Rose

Fragrant Rose has her own spot in the garden. Never hurt by her own thorns, she daintily clambers about her plant picking away the old petals from her flowers. She chooses the softest of these to dress herself in. All the fairies in Flower Fairyland love Rose and have a special song to sing her when they visit the rose garden. Rose is always flattered when she hears this song and gives her friends gifts of rose water to say thank you.

Best and dearest flower that grows,

Perfect both to see and smell

Words can never, never tell

Half the beauty of a Rose –

Buds that open to disclose

Fold on fold of purest white,

Lovely pink, or red that glows

Deep, sweet-scented. What delight

To be Fairy of the Rose!

Lavender

Lavender washes and scents the clothes for many of the Flower Fairies. She is the sweetest fairy, who never says no to scrubbing the fairies' outfits. Lavender makes soap for the fairies' bathtime and perfumes for the girls.

Burning sprigs of lavender keeps naughty elves away!

Elder's lacy dress is delicate to wash

Pear Blossom is happy that his jacket is freshly washed

26

Christmas Tree's dress must
sparkle and glitter

Flower's shoes
... extra scrubbing

Climbing makes
Sycamore's
clothes grubby

27

Poppy

Poppy is one of the oldest fairies and enjoys arranging parties and other treats for the fairy children. In the summer, when her poppies are in full bloom, Poppy invites all the baby fairies over to her plant. She sits them all inside one of the fluffy blossoms and offers them bowls of poppy seeds, which is just like popcorn for fairies!

Poplar shares his seeds with Double Daisy

What is little Deadnettle up to?

Baby Apple Blossom eats till she is full

Poppy's friend, Fuchsia drops in to join in the fun

Mulberry giggles

Baby Kingcup thinks Fuchsia is a very dainty guest

Snapdragon

Bees love to visit flowers and fairies in the garden and they are especially
pleased to visit Snapdragon. They dive straight into Snapdragon's blossoms
until their bodies are hidden and then sip at the nectar inside. When the bees
have drank as much as they can, they reverse out of the flower back end first!
Snapdragon himself looks upon all this with fondness and if he
sees a bee that's shy, he hails him with a song:

Snapdragon's name is only a game-
It isn't as fierce as it sounds;
The Snapdragon Elf is pleased as punch
When bumble comes on his rounds!

Red Clover likes to watch the bees with Snapdragon

Yellow Nettle flits above the plants

This little fairy likes to bother bumble bees!

31

Sweet Pea

All the fairy babies in the garden love Sweet Pea, especially the girls.
Sweet Pea has a fabulous collection of outfits that she likes
to dress the babies up in, just as if they were dolls! Sweet Pea
fairy has a little sister, whom she spoils with all of her best
dressing-up clothes. When little Sweet Pea grows up,
she will be the most fashionable fairy around!

Flouncy collars and sleeves are just the thing

Petal petticoats are perfect for fairy balls

Velvety blue petals feel soft and cosy against fairy skin

Dainty blossoms adorn a petal skirt

A delicate lacy dress to impress the Fairy Queen

Does it suit you, Baby?
Yes, I really think
Nothing's more becoming
Than this pretty pink!

33

Nasturtium

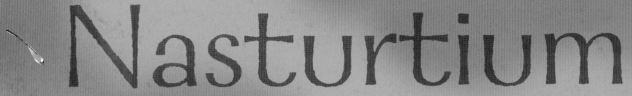

When it's time for a Fairy Banquet, Nasturtium's flat leaves make perfect plates. When spring rain appears, Nasturtium lends out his leaves to the other fairies to use as umbrellas. When the hot summer sun shines down, Nasturtium's leaves make perfect circles of shade. But when the winter snow blows in, Nasturtium is sleeping and nowhere to be found.

Nasturtium the jolly,
O ho, O ho!
He holds up his brolly
Just so, just so!

Bird's Foot Trefoil leads a
merry dance in the

Heather follows close behind, although she would rather take the lead

Pansy keeps to the rear, making sure the little ones don't go astray

Heather

Heather is a tomboy fairy who loves to run around, dropping seeds everywhere! She is one of the most active fairies in the garden and doesn't like to sit still for very long. When she *is* sitting quietly, Heather uses the springy leaves from her plant to make soft beds for the baby fairies. And her stalks make perfect brooms for cleaning up with.

Ho, jolly me! From east to west, the moorland waits to be dressed.

Baby Forget-me-not lies on a bed of heather

I come, I come! With footsteps sure, I run to clothe the waiting moor.

Iris

If there is a pond or a stream in the garden, then Iris will settle near it. Iris teaches the garden fairies how to swim, as some of them are so afraid of water that they do not even dare fly over!
Iris has a pretty voice that tinkles just like a stream and from time to time she can be heard singing her song:

I am Iris: I'm the daughter, of the marshland and the water.

Looking down, I see the gleam, of the clear and peaceful stream

Water-lilies large and fair, with their leaves are floating there

All the water-world I see, and my own face smiles at me!

Mallow is too scared to go near the water

Sycamore dips his toe in the water

Iris speaks gently to Sycamore, telling him not to be afraid

39

Honeysuckle

Of all the Flower Fairies, Honeysuckle climbs the best. He can scramble up walls, trees, and even hedges! As he climbs, Honeysuckle pulls the leafy tendrils of his plant with him. In the evening, Honeysuckle climbs up to the very top of his plant, and plucks one of the blossoms. He blows into the flower as hard as he can to spread his honeysuckle scent into the night sky. Night moths are attracted to the smell and come from far and wide to drink honeysuckle nectar.

The lane is deep, the band is steep,
The tangled hedge is high,
And clinging, twisting, up I creep,
And climb towards the sky.
The people in the lane below
Look up and see me there,
Where I my honey-trumpets blow,
Whose sweetness fills the air.

Nightshade

In the shadows at the very bottom of the garden, lives the Nightshade fairy. He spends his time polishing his gleaming red and green berries so they look pretty. But this plant is dangerous and luckily, high above, the other Flower Fairies rattle their branches to warn children to stay away. If this doesn't work, Beechnut and Chestnut drop their conkers and nuts to the ground to distract any children who might be passing!

Chestnut keeps watch

Beechnut throws her seeds

My name is Nightshade, also Bittersweet

Ah, little folk, be wise!

Hide you your hands behind you when we meet,

Turn you away your eyes.

My flowers you shall not pick, nor berries eat,

For in them poison lies.

Spindle Berry waits

Michaelmas Daisy

As night falls in the garden, some Flower Fairies become more lively. Many have been asleep under their plants all day – they prefer the cool stillness of the night to the heat of the day. To help the night fairies tend their plants and play in the dark, Michaelmas Daisy sprinkles fairy dust into the yellow middles of his flowers. The gleaming blossoms become lanterns lighting up the tiny fairy paths around the garden and allowing the fairies to see what they are doing.

Bindweed admires the sparkly michaelmas lights

Labernum and Elderberry snooze in the dusk